Story play™

This book belongs to

_____.

This book was read by

_____

on

_____.

Are you ready to start reading the **StoryPlay** way?

Read the story on its own. Play the activities together
as you read!

Ready. Set. Smart!

TO OWEN SAMUEL AND KEI SCARLETT BERNSTEIN

Text and illustrations copyright © 2010 by Mark Teague
Prompts and activities copyright © 2017 by Scholastic Inc.

Scholastic Inc., 557 Broadway, New York, NY 10012
Scholastic UK Ltd., Euston House, 24 Eversholt Street, London NW1 1DB

Library of Congress Cataloging-in-Publication Data available
ISBN 978-1-338-18159-3
10 9 8 7 6 5 4 3 2 1   17 18 19 20 21
Printed in Panyu, China   137
This edition first printing, September 2017
Book design by Doan Buu

BY MARK TEAGUE

FIREHOUSE!

CARTWHEEL BOOKS • AN IMPRINT OF SCHOLASTIC INC.

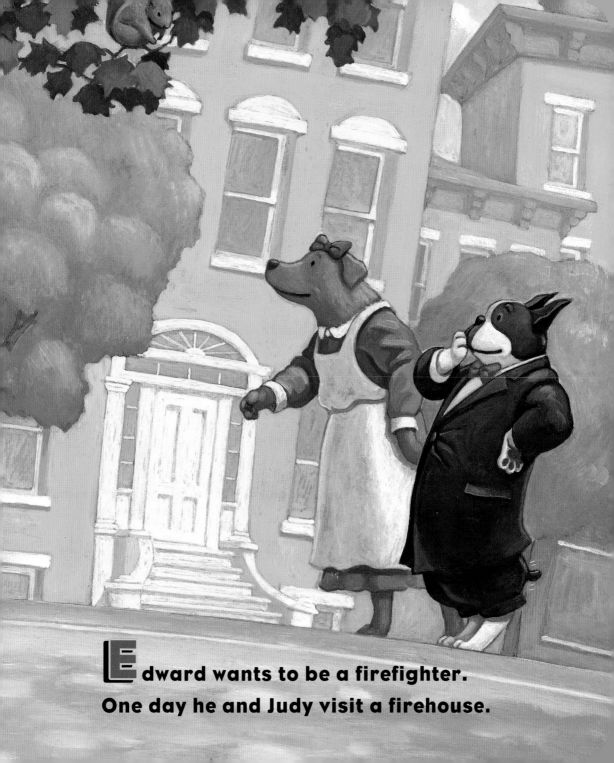

Edward wants to be a firefighter.
One day he and Judy visit a firehouse.

Edward tries on a shiny red fire hat.

Mrs. Speckle, the fire chief, shows them around.
"First you can help wash the fire truck," she says.
"Later we will have a practice fire drill."

Is the hat too big or too small for Edward? How can you tell?

Everyone helps.
"A clean fire engine is a happy fire engine,"
says a firefighter.
Edward climbs into the driver's seat.
He steers to the right. He steers to the left.

"This is where we live,"
says a firefighter.

Edward and Judy are playing cards when the fire alarm goes off. What are the other firefighters doing?

"This is a fire drill," calls
the fire chief.
The firefighters spring into action!

Have you ever practiced a fire drill?
What do you remember doing?

Everyone hurries down the fire pole.

"Hang on, Edward!" a firefighter calls.
The fire engine speeds away.

Judy opens the fire hydrant.

The water is so strong it knocks Edward off his feet.

Everyone works together.

Edward practices going up the ladder.

But he needs help coming down.

Lifesaving is a firefighter's most important job.

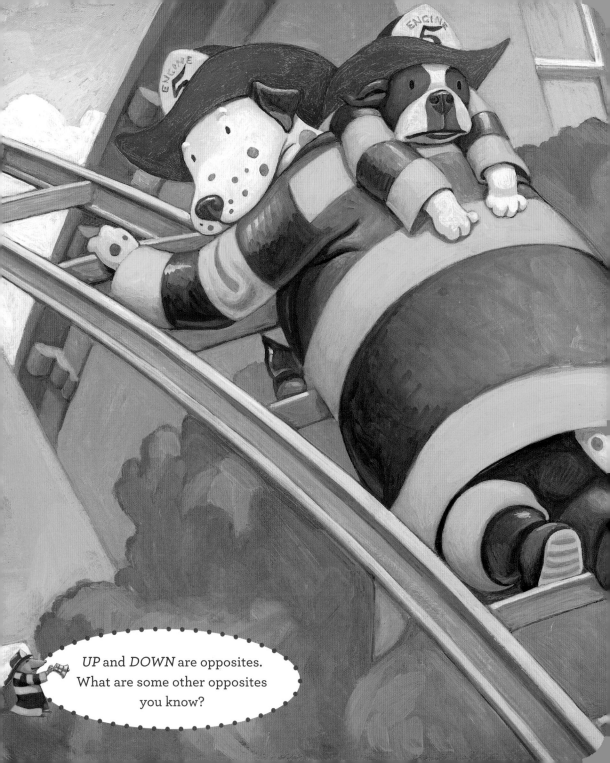

UP and DOWN are opposites.
What are some other opposites
you know?

What are the firefighters eating for lunch? What is your favorite food to eat at lunchtime?

They return to the firehouse.
After lunch, the alarm rings again.
This time, it is a real emergency!

A kitten is stuck up a tree!
"Who will save her?" asks a firefighter.
Edward volunteers, "Let me!"

Can you find the kitten that is stuck in the tree? How do you think Edward will save the cat?

Edward climbs the ladder and rescues the kitten.
"Good work!" the firefighters cheer.

Edward saves the day.

There is a big parade to celebrate.

A firefighter needs rest.

It is bedtime at the

Story time fun never ends with these creative activities!

★ When I Grow Up . . . ★

Edward wants to be a firefighter when he grows up. He visits a firehouse to learn about this job. He helps wash the fire truck, climbs a ladder, and saves a kitten from a tree. What do you want to be when you grow up? It's time to explore!

When I grow up I want to be a . . .
I want to do this because . . .
This job would make me feel . . .

Now pick another job, and do the exercise all over again!

★ Hero of the Story ★

A hero is someone who does something brave or good. In the story, Edward is a hero when he saves the cat that is stuck in the tree. Can you think of a time when someone you know was a hero? Tell a story about how that person saved the day!